ADVENTURES OF A
CREEPER

Mervyn, the creeper who wanted to burn bright!

Silver Dolphin

Silver Dolphin Books
An imprint of Printers Row Publishing Group
A division of Readerlink Distribution Services, LLC
10350 Barnes Canyon Road, Suite 100, San Diego, CA 92121
www.silverdolphinbooks.com

Printers Row Publishing Group is a division of Readerlink Distribution Services, LLC.
Silver Dolphin Books is a registered trademark of Readerlink Distribution Services, LLC.

Translated from the French, *Moi, le Creeper*, by Daria Chernysheva

All notations of errors or omissions should be addressed to Silver Dolphin Books, Editorial Department, at the above address. All other correspondence (author inquiries, permissions) concerning the content of this book should be addressed to:
404 éditions
c/o Édi8
12 avenue d'Italie
75013 Paris, France
www.lisez.com/404-éditions/24

ISBN: 978-1-68412-922-5
Manufactured, printed, and assembled in Crawfordsville, Indiana, USA
LSC/03/19
23 22 21 20 19   1 2 3 4 5

ADVENTURES OF A
CREEPER

Mervyn, the creeper who wanted to burn bright!

Written by *Books Kid*
Introduction by *Aypierre*
Translated from the French by *Daria Chernysheva*
Illustrated by *Elliot Gaudard*

Silver Dolphin

INTRODUCTION FROM AYPIERRE

I remember the first time I met a creeper.

Back then, I was still discovering Minecraft and I wasn't making any videos. I didn't know anything about the game, and I was already having a hard time handling my wooden axe and my blocks of dirt.

I had managed to build my very first shelter (which had no roof and no windows) so that I had somewhere to spend the night. Then I saw something through the door. Even though I was a beginner, I knew to avoid skeletons, zombies, and spiders, because they are all very common enemies in the world of video games. But, without thinking, I opened the door to my unexpected guest: a funny green creature with a strange expression. And then, this happened:

"PSSSSSSSHHHHHHHHHH BOoM!!!!!!"

It was the first in a long series of explosions.

I quickly learned to fear these diabolical monsters and to always remain alert, listening for that alarming whistling sound that often comes right before "Game Over."

Multiple creepers pursued me back to my shelter. I screamed in surprise when I came face-to-face with one of them in a cave. I yelled angrily when my beautiful structure was deformed by a series of chain explosions. In short, the creepers had quickly become my nightmare, and I hurriedly learned the famous "hit-and-run-away" method of dealing with them.

That's how it is with creepers! A creeper swiftly latches on to people and doesn't know how to show his love in any other way except by exploding under the nose of the player unfortunate enough to have attracted his attention. However, the creeper is also the game's mascot, and I've lost count of the merchandise that proudly displays the "terrifying" face of our favorite monster.

So, I ask the following question:

IS THE CREEPER A PRANK-LOVING MONSTER, OR A MISUNDERSTOOD CREATURE?

Today, this book allows us to discover Mervyn's story. While I was reading it, I laughed a lot and grew fond of this little guy. Let's hope his story will help us better understand creepers so we can all live in harmony! In any case, I am sure you will enjoy the unexpected twists and humor this story has to offer.

As for me, I'm going back to my adventures and wish you all a pleasant read. And who knows? Maybe I'll also succeed in becoming best friends with a cree...

"PSSSSSSSHHHHHHHHH BOoM!!!!!!"

DAY 1

Dear Diary,

I think I should begin by introducing myself. My name is Mervyn and I've decided to keep a diary to help me prepare for the Creeper Combustion and Confusion Competition.

What? You didn't think that creepers kept private diaries? Well, I've got one. Because I do know how to read and write, thank you very much. I don't know why people think creepers are stupid. If they listened to us, they would know that we are communicating with them.

The thing is, we all have a little hair on our tongues, and so this makes it sound like we're hissing all the time—like sssssssssnakes. We also speak very fast. I think I can see why it sounds like hissing, if you're not listening closely. But it's not.

In fact, we're saying:

"Hey! We want to be your friends!"

Then, we become so frustrated at not being understood that we explode. It's very annoying. Anyway.

THE CREEPER COMBUSTION AND CONFUSION COMPETITION.

You must be wondering what this is. Well,

everything is in the name. Every year, the cr
organize a championship to see who can crea
most disorder and destruction. My dad won three
times in a row before withdrawing because of an
unfortunate accident involving an ocelot, a carrot,
and a large bucket of lava.

Believe me, you don't want to know.
As you can imagine, there's a lot of pressure on
me to be as good as my dad, who broke all the
records with his accomplishments. This stress is
enough to make any creeper explode.

So, I've decided to keep a diary to track my
training progress. If I can find a new and awesome
way to cause maximum damage, victory will be
mine. But it will have to be something really
incredible. Wesley goes on and on bragging about his
ideas and saying that he's on fire.

Ha, ha ! He's on fire...

Get it?

DAY 2

Have I already told you that I hate Wesley?

He's way too full of himself and is so convinced he's going to win the competition, that he says there's no need for the rest of us "losers" to even show up.

Wesley is going down

Wesley says he's going to do so much damage that this will be the end of the Creeper Combustion and Confusion Competition—because nobody will ever be able to come close to him. He says that even my dad, with his records, will see Wesley's performance and then look like a baby creeper who's trying to explode for the first time but can't, and runs away to the forest to cry. Now that's going too far.

NOBODY MAKES MY DAD CRY.

I've been thinking about what sort of unexpected stuff I could come up with. I absolutely have to surprise the judges. I have to do something that will go down in creeper history. It's a lot of pressure, being the son of Big Raymundo, but I know I can do it.

If Wesley thinks he can dominate the championship, it's because he hasn't seen anything yet. Me, I'm going to explode. In every sense of the word.

DAY 3

My dad came by to help me train. I gave all that I had to impress him. I'm working really hard and I want to show him that I'm doing my best. First, I launched myself into a tree and exploded just before I hit it. The tree fell and took down the two trees next to it.

After I respawned, I ran to my dad. "Hey Dad! What do you think? That was cool, right?"

My dad furrowed his eyebrows. "If you had exploded over here, you would have done twice as much damage."

He went to the place he was pointing to and blew himself up. He was right. He destroyed six trees with one tiny explosion. Why hadn't I done that?

He came back to me as he respawned.

"Remember, the judges will not only observe the scope of the damage you cause. They will also take your creativity and originality into account, with respect to everything you do within the given time. Everyone knows the trick of making trees fall. Everyone has seen it a million times. If you think you're going to win by running around the whole forest and bringing down trees—then you better stay out of the competition. That's a classic rookie mistake. Frankly, Mervyn, I thought you'd grown out of this kind of childish play."

I hate it when my dad looks at me like this. You know what it's like. A look that says, "My boy, you're letting me down a lot. If only Wesley were my son."

"I'm sorry, Dad," I sighed. "I'll try to do better."
I examined the clearing around me (because it was a clearing now that we had destroyed all the trees).

"Hey, I have an idea!"

I went to the stream. I observed the water and carefully selected my point of destruction.

"Look, Dad!"

BOOM!

I tried to make the biggest explosion possible. When the dust had settled, I looked around, expecting to see an enormous waterfall.

"Oh no! It didn't work!" I said, making a face, when I realized that all I had achieved was to widen the stream a little. I had thought that the water would gush out into the forest and sweep half the earth away, creating a pretty waterfall.

My dad rejoined me, shaking his head. "Mervyn, Mervyn, Mervyn. You need to have better judgment. What do they teach you in creeper school these days? You know that the river water is stagnant here. It doesn't flow. All that you have done is make a hole in the ground—or, to put it better, a small dent. You can hardly call that a hole. If I were a judge, you could count yourself lucky if I awarded you even one point. The competition is approaching. I hoped that you would have understood all this a while ago."

"But, Dad," I moaned, "I'm trying. Can't you help me a little? If you could show me how you destroyed that main road . . . "

"I've already explained to you, Mervyn: If you imitate me, not only will they take points away from you, but you will also be disqualified." My dad sighed. "This whole thing wasn't a good idea. Certain things cannot be taught. Destruction is a basic instinct that all creepers are supposed to have. It's this feeling you get in your stomach just before an explosion, when you know that you will destroy everything around you. And, afterward, you don't even need to look around to check how much damage you have done—because you

CREEPER

BOOM

TNT

EXPLOSION

19

know that your target has been destroyed."

I nodded as if I knew what he was talking about, but, to be honest, I didn't have a clue. I had never felt that. The only time my stomach had ever spoken to me was when I had food poisoning after I ate some rotten flesh a zombie had dropped. I had been sick for days.

"Let's face the facts, Mervyn. There is only one champion in the family. Maybe you should pass on the competition this year. Train harder and enter next year. You don't want to look ridiculous, right?"

"I'm not going to look ridiculous! I can do this, Dad!" I felt my body trembling. I needed to control myself, or else I was going to explode in my dad's face.

He didn't like it when that happened to me. Last time, he told me, his nose had been itchy for days.

"Are you sure?" Dad threw me a skeptical look before he vanished into the forest.

Although he technically did come by to help me train, I would have liked it if he could have helped me train for real.

DAY 4

After my dad's visit yesterday, I felt too discouraged to practice my explosions today. What's the point, when your own father thinks that you have no chance of winning?

Wesley was probably right. They should just give him the crown and then we can all go home.

I wandered in the forest without paying attention to where I was going. I was lost in my thoughts and I didn't even notice when I left the forest and began walking across the plains. I saw a village directly ahead and decided to go blow up a few houses. Maybe this would lift my spirits again.

"Aah! Aah! A creeper! HELP!"

Usually, the screams of terrified villagers bring a smile back to my face, but today I was too depressed to appreciate them.

I roamed through the village streets, feeling gloomy, while the villagers ran all around me. Soon the iron golems would arrive to chase me away, so I didn't have much time if I wanted to destroy something.

A building caught my attention. I went closer to read what was written over the door.

"LIBRARY"

The library! This gave me an idea. Maybe I could find a book inside that would help me with the competition.

I walked through the door. The librarian screamed and rushed outside the instant he saw me. I ignored him.

I was on a mission.

I browsed the aisles in search of a book that could be useful to me. I came upon a section titled "Creeperology" and looked over all the books on the shelves.

How to Defuse a Creeper

10 Practical Tips for Fighting Creepers

The Creepers that I Knew and Killed

The Best Traps for Creepers

They were of no interest to me. I should have simply blown up the library.

And that's when I saw them. Books about construction and crafting. But of course! How to do the most damage possible? By making tools of destruction!

I quickly gathered all the books I could carry (I even stuffed one in my mouth). Then I left and plunged back into the forest.

It was really tempting to blow up the library before leaving, just because, but that could wait for another time. I had a lot of things on my plate now.

DAY 5

If my dad could see how hard I worked, studying these books all day long, he would be proud. Well ... either he would be proud, or he would want to know why I didn't usually try so hard at creeper school.

I had no idea you could make so much cool stuff! You could build far more than just shelters. You could construct whole cities!

My mind was whirling after all this reading. What if I dropped out of the competition and simply went somewhere to build the first creeper city?

Then I thought of Wesley, who makes fun of me all the time. No, I am going to wipe that smile off his face once and for all.

After I finished all the books, I began at the

beginning again, and reread them all. They had so much information in them that I had trouble remembering it all. I will have to start taking notes and putting together a plan.

For the time being, I hid my books near a tree in a little hole that I dug and then covered up, so no one could find them. I don't want Wesley to steal my ideas. I will win this competition, and the next, and the next, and the next. If somebody is going to beat my dad's record, it will be me.

DAY 6

"Whatcha doing there, worm?"

I raised my head. Wesley was standing over me, jeering with two of his friends. Just my luck! I thought I had found a quiet little corner in the schoolyard to sit and think about how I was going to tackle the championship. I should have known that Wesley wouldn't leave me in peace.

"I'm just thinking, that's all."

"No, that's not possible. You need a brain to think! You wouldn't look so blank if you had something in your head!"

Wesley and his two friends burst out laughing. I started to shake and had to steady myself. We're not supposed to blow each other up in the schoolyard. Not because they're worried that creepers are going to get hurt, no. But because it's a lot of work for the janitors to constantly be repairing the holes we make in the ground.

Mr. Jungle spends his time ranting, at any rate. And it's worse when he's sweeping up the dust.

I was beginning to get sick of this. I'd had enough of Wesley making fun of me.

"You know, for someone who is convinced he's going to win the competition, you spend a lot of time trying to discourage me. One might say you're afraid of losing. What's up, Wes? You scared?"

Wesley paled, and I knew I had struck a nerve. "That's Wesley to you, worm. And I'm not scared of anything."

"Oh, yeah?" I raised an eyebrow. "And that's Mervyn to you. And if you're not scared, then it wouldn't hurt you to place a little bet."

"Go on, what is it?"

"If you beat me in the championship, I will do your homework for a month. But if I beat you, then you do mine."

Wesley burst out laughing. "Is that all? Then it's a deal! I hate doing my homework, anyway."

"No, that's not all."

Now this was definitely stupid, but I wanted to wipe that smirk off his face at all costs.

"That bet was only about which one of us does better in the competition. If one of us actually wins, then the other has to wear a T-shirt with **'I AM A HUGE LOSER'** written on it. Then he has to go around the forest—no running—while shouting, 'I am a loser!' and give out rotten fruit to people so they can throw it at him."

Wesley probably wouldn't have accepted if his friends hadn't been there, but I know he didn't want to lose face in front of them.

"I hope you're stocked up on fruits, worm. You're going to need them! Come on, guys. Let's go to the explosion field to train a bit. We'll show this loser how it's done."

Wesley and his friends left in the direction of the explosion field, leaving me standing there, trembling.

What have I done? Now I will <u>have</u> to win.
Wesley in that T-shirt—I can't miss that!

DAY 7

"MERVYN! PAY ATTENTION!"

Mr. Bing, our gym teacher, yelled at me from over my head. It made me jump, and the other students giggled.

"Very good, Mervyn," said Mr. Bing. "You volunteered to go first. Today we're doing the obstacle course."

I grumbled as I dragged my feet to the starting line.

"Don't forget, this is good training for the championship. I want to see neat explosions and quick respawns. You are all going to be timed, and the slowest creeper is going to have to do the whole course again. Are you ready? Set, go!"

He blew his whistle and I launched myself toward the first obstacle. Except that, because I was anxious to do really well, I tripped on a root and sprawled flat on my face.

Everybody laughed, Wesley louder than the others.

"You have no chance in the competition!"

I got up, but my knee hurt and I couldn't run as fast as I usually do. I got to the end at last, but it took me nearly five minutes, and I knew it would take a miracle for someone to go slower than me.

There was no miracle. All the others completed the course and Wesley even took the time to stick out his tongue at me before exploding at the finish line.

"Well done, Wesley!" Mr. Bing congratulated him. "That's your best time yet. I'm looking forward to seeing your moves in the competition. You will make this school proud."
"Thanks, Mr. Bing," Wesley replied, smiling and showing all his teeth. "I can run even faster."

"I'm sure of it. However, it is Mr. Mervyn here who has to run faster. Go ahead, Mervyn. You were the slowest and you know what that means. I want to see you improve your time— or else you're going to detention."

I took a deep breath to calm myself as I stood at the starting line. I could not get detention. I had too much work to do before the competition. On the bright side, my first time had been so bad, it surely couldn't get any worse...

Yeah, well. It turns out that, yes, I can, in fact, do worse. As soon as I started to run, Wesley hollered at me:

"YOU'RE GOING TO LOSE, WORM!"

This upset me so much that I exploded—which earned me a penalty in time. And I was so annoyed that I did not respawn correctly: I ended up with one foot inside out and this slowed me down even more.

When I crossed the finish line, hobbling, I didn't need to look at Mr. Bing to know I was going to detention.

"Congratulations, Mervyn."

What? Had I somehow managed to beat my old time, anyway?

"You've succeeded in setting the most disastrous time of the year. I am disappointed. I'm ashamed that my students could be this bad. You're going to detention until the end of the week."

"Until the end of the week?" I repeated. I couldn't believe it. My dad was going to kill me! "But," I pleaded, "Mr. Bing ..."

Wesley shoved me as soon as we went back to the locker room. "I told you you were a loser."

I was too upset to care about Wesley. How was I going to train for the competition if I had to spend every afternoon with Mr. Bing?

DAY 8

"Okay, Mervyn. Once I'm done with you, you'll never finish last in an obstacle course."

I grumbled as Mr. Bing led me to the start of the course.

"You're going to go around, then around, then around again, until you don't know which way is up and which is down. And then you'll start over! So, take your mark ... Go!"

I remained standing on the spot, unsure of whether I should give it my all or go easy at the beginning. I couldn't believe I had to run in circles for hours. It was exhausting just thinking about it.

"What are you waiting for, Mervyn? I said:

GO, GO, GO!"

Mr. Bing began to run behind me, which left me with no choice but to go as fast as possible.

"Choose the right moment for your explosions. They will help you cover more ground in the course!" advised Mr. Bing. "And ... now!"

I blew up right when he told me to, and, once I'd respawned, I realized that Mr. Bing was right. The force of the explosion had propelled me further along the course and I was now much closer to the next obstacle.

"Well done, Mervyn. One more time!
Explode ... now!"

I did as he said, and, when I arrived at the finish line, I had achieved the best time of my entire life.

"Good, Mervyn. It is nice to see you put some effort into my class, for a change. It's a shame it had to come to detention for you to get here. Very good. Now, back to the start."

"Again?"

I was wiped out, but Mr. Bing was relentless. True to his word, he made me go around and around and around the obstacle course, until I had cramps in my feet and my head hurt from exploding so often.

"Excellent. That's enough for now," Mr. Bing finally decreed. "Same time, same place tomorrow."

"Yes, Mr. Bing," I replied, gasping for air.

In that moment, I was mad at Mr. Bing for making me sweat like this. But I do have to admit that my exploding abilities had greatly improved, and all in the space of just one evening.

Maybe it was a good thing to get stuck with detention, after all.

DAY 9

I never would have thought that one day I would look forward to going to detention, but I admit that I was impatiently waiting for school to end so I could get back to the obstacle course with Mr. Bing.

When I arrived, the course looked completely different.

"Right, Mervyn. Since you managed so well yesterday, I've decided to make things a little more interesting. I've created a more complex course, and you're going to attempt it by yourself while I evaluate your progress. Then we'll take it from there."

I got into position, ready to go. I was going to complete the obstacle course as fast as I could and show Mr. Bing how much I had improved.

"TAKE YOUR MARK ... GET SET ... GO!"

I launched myself forward, and, for once, I didn't end up sprawled across the ground. *Step one: check!*

I was going to (crush) everything!

I turned a corner and found myself face-to-face with an enormous pile of iron. I was going far too fast to go around it or go over it, so I had no choice. I exploded.

Once I'd respawned, I realized that the force of the blast had thrown me backward. I now had to run even further to get back to the course and I had lost a lot of time. I gritted my teeth and sped up as much as I could to try to make up for the lost time—but then I came to a slope with a lot of twists and turns.

I had to zigzag between tall poles. Toward the end, however, the last two poles were so close together that I couldn't slip between them.

BOOM !

Once again, I exploded and was thrown backward along the obstacle course. I scattered in all directions: one of my feet landed up on the top of a pole! I had to climb the pole in order to get it back. I felt time slipping away from me. This wasn't going to do.

I ended up crossing the finish line by creeping along the ground, exhausted. Mr. Bing shook his head as he stopped his watch.

"What happened, Mervyn? That was a terrible time!"

"It was because of the new obstacles," I protested. "I didn't have a choice! I had to blow them up and this slowed me down."

"Yes, that was the thing to do—but you should have used these explosions to your advantage. The obstacle course has supposedly been designed to test you, but there is always a shortcut if you know how to look for it. Come and see."

I followed Mr. Bing to the starting line and we walked to the first obstacle, which Mr. Bing had reconstructed.

"When you turned this corner," said Mr. Bing, "you saw the iron blocks and you panicked. Don't panic! You have time to breathe and think about the best line of attack. If you had been positioned here, you would have

been able to launch yourself over. Look."
He exploded to show me what he meant.
And he was right. He overcame the obstacle
and landed far
ahead on the
other side.

"Your turn,
go on."

He restacked
the metal and
I went to the
spot Mr. Bing
was pointing at.

"Face the blocks,"
Mr. Bing specified.
"When you are
ready, explode."

I did as he said:
I closed my eyes and exploded.

"It worked!" I said, delighted. "It really worked!"

"Indeed," Mr. Bing acknowledged. "Let's now go to the next stage in the obstacle course. Let's see if you can find the best place to position yourself."

DAY 10

Today was my last day of detention. In fact, I'm pretty sad about it. Mr. Bing has helped me in these past few days in a way that my dad never has. I've really learned some useful things for the competition.

"Alright, Mervyn. Today, I'm going to have you attempt a number of different obstacle courses. This way, before every obstacle, you will have to choose the best position to be sure of aiming straight."

"Yes, Mr. Bing."
I stepped up to the starting line. I was determined not to let Mr. Bing down.

My first attempt was not an overwhelming success.

"I'm sorry, Mr. Bing," I gasped, as I crossed the finish line. "I did my best. But I guess I'm just not good enough."

"Don't say that, Mervyn. Never say that. I never want to hear those words from your mouth again. You have it in you. I've seen it. You just have to believe it. Alright, I'm going to set up a new course. Every time you get to a new obstacle, I want you to ask yourself: 'What would Mr. Bing do?' Don't forget that you have time to think about what you're going to do. You don't have to explode the instant you arrive at an obstacle."

"Yes, Mr. Bing."

"Excellent. Alright, take your mark ... get set ... go!"

"What would Mr. Bing do?
What would Mr. Bing do?"

These words bounced around my head as I attacked the obstacle course.

The first obstacle was a barricade. My first

reaction was to explode, but, instead of doing that, I stopped. Then I ran forward to jump over the barricade.

It worked! I overcame it in a single leap and I landed a few feet further along. If I had exploded, I would still be respawning. Instead, I advanced toward the next stage.

The next obstacle was even more difficult: a jumble of wooden planks, iron bars, and blocks of dirt.

"What would Mr. Bing do?" I murmured. And then, I had an idea. I charged straight at the obstacle, catapulted into the air, and exploded the instant I was at the highest point. The force of the explosion projected me far onto the other side. Once more, I had cut a sizable length off the course.

I couldn't believe it! I was going to achieve the best time of my entire life in the most difficult obstacle course I had ever done.

"Well done, Mervyn!" Mr. Bing congratulated me as I crossed the finish line. He had a smile on his face. "That was an excellent time. You can join the school obstacle course team if you keep this up."

"Seriously, Mr. Bing? You think so?"

"Of course. I know talent when I see it. I always knew you could perform better than you do in class. You just needed some encouragement."

"Thank you, Mr. Bing. I know detention isn't supposed to be fun, but I had a great time this week with you."

"Well ... I know what it's like to have a famous father," said Mr. Bing. He paused, wondering if he should tell me. "My father is Eric Bing."

"Eric Bing!" I exclaimed. "The obstacle course champion?"

"The very same," he admitted.

Everyone had heard of Eric Bing. He held the speed record in obstacle courses. He had represented our forest in international championships and had been ready to win his fourth title when a terrible accident involving a zombie pigman, a glistening melon, and redstone ore had put an end to his career.

Believe me, you don't want to know.

"I was never as talented as my father in obstacle courses, so I became a gym teacher. But you ... I see the same spark in you as in your father. You can become a true champion. You just have to believe in yourself."

A small tear escaped from the corner of my eye. If only my dad could hear Mr. Bing.

"Thank you, Mr. Bing."

It was the only thing I could manage to say.

DAY 11

After all that intense work with Mr. Bing
this week, I am really determined to win the
competition. Mr. Bing showed me that I am
capable of it. I simply have to develop an
unbeatable strategy, and the gold medal is mine.

I went back to the place where I had buried
my books. But dig as I might the books were
nowhere to be found.

Maybe I had forgotten exactly where I had left
them. I thought they were under the tree to
the left of the lake, but maybe I was wrong.

I started to dig around every tree, but still
no books.

"Looking for these?"

I turned around and saw Wesley, holding my books!

"You think you're going to win the competition by reading books? You're even dumber than you look."

"Give them back!"

I rushed at Wesley, but he raised the books so high I couldn't grab them.

"Hey, relax," snickered Wesley. "I am going to give them to you. But you'll have to fetch them."

He threw the books into the water.

"My books!"

Wesley burst out laughing and disappeared into the forest, while I splashed into the lake to try to save the books.

By the time I had gathered them all, they were ruined.

I could have cried. These books were the key to my victory. How was I going to come up with a genius plan now?

DAY 12

Wesley had left me no choice. I had to return to the village to look for other books.

I set out, thinking it shouldn't take me long to gather everything I needed, now that I knew where the library was.

But, when I got to the village, I noticed that the villagers had summoned more iron golems to protect the place. This wasn't fair. I hadn't destroyed anything the last time I went to the library. I only wanted some books, but I knew the golems wouldn't listen to me.

"Think, Mervyn, think! What would Mr. Bing do?"

And then I knew.

It was just like an obstacle course! I sneaked around the village to the other side. I chose precisely the right place, calculated the angles, and then I blew myself up.

BOOM !

As I'd hoped, the iron golems ran in the direction of the explosion. I had selected the perfect place and landed precisely in front of the library. I didn't have a lot of time, so I respawned quickly and slipped inside.

"A creeper! Aaaah!"

I ignored the librarian, who ran away screaming. But I knew I didn't have much time. He was going to come back with iron golems.

Luckily, I knew what I was looking for. I headed to the "Crafting" section. Most of the books I had taken last time had been replaced, so I grabbed my favorites and two or three new ones.

On a sudden whim, I also took one about setting traps for creepers—just in case there was something in it that could be useful against Wesley. Then I set out for the forest to hide my treasure in a safe place.

DAY 13

I read the instruction manual on setting traps for creepers. If I could capture Wesley for just one day, I would have some peace and would be able to concentrate on getting ready for the championship.

The only problem was that most of these traps were designed to kill creepers. I didn't want to kill Wesley. He may be a complete pain in the butt, but that would be going too far.

However, there was one trap I really liked. You construct a little room with doors and you lure the creeper in. Then you lock the doors after him, and, bam, he's trapped!

It didn't look too hard to make, and once I'd gotten the idea into my head I couldn't think of anything else. I began to gather the necessary materials to build the trap. It was a bit difficult, not having arms, but I quickly figured out how to transport things by using my feet. Also, it's crazy how easy it is to move stuff if you blow up in the right spot.

It took me a while, but, in the end, I had everything I needed. I began to place blocks and doors in their proper places so I could trap Wesley. When I was done, I stepped back to admire my handiwork.

"Whatcha making, worm?"
Wesley! Exactly the person I wanted. This saved me from having to find a way to lure him here. "I'm just building a little thing to help me train for the competition."

I tried to keep my voice light. I had to be careful with Wesley. He was suspicious, and I had to find the right words to make him step into my trap.

"Oh yeah? I'd say these are some stupid doors

that lead nowhere. How does it work?"

I couldn't believe it! Wesley was making it easy for me! If I could lure him inside, then I could duck around him, double-lock the doors, and run away.

"I'll show you."

I opened the door and I stepped into the trap. "Got you!"

I spun around and saw Wesley slam the door

shut! He pressed himself against it to keep it closed.

I turned to the other doors, but Wesley's friends had quietly sneaked up while we were talking, and now they blocked all the exits. I had wanted to trap Wesley—and he had trapped me instead!

I heard the bolts scraping in the doors as Wesley locked them one by one so that I couldn't escape. Then he threw the key into the bushes.

"Later, worm! Good luck getting out!"

Wesley and his friends drummed on the doors before they ran away, leaving me stuck there, caught in my own trap.

DAY 14

IT TOOK ME FOREVER TO GET OUT OF THAT TRAP!

On the bright side, the book had been right: the trap is very effective for capturing creepers.

It was my dad who finally heard my cries for help and came to rescue me. He wasn't very happy. He kept asking me how I could be so foolish, and what could have possibly been going through my head when I decided to construct a creeper trap.

I decided to not tell him I was going to build other things, that the trap was only the beginning.

DAY 15

Sometimes, I would like to have a best friend. I, too, want somebody with whom I can share all my secrets. That's why I'm glad to have started this diary. It's a space where I can talk about my thoughts and feelings without anybody making fun of me.

If I try to talk about what I'm thinking with the other kids at school, they laugh at me, and in return I get:

"Mervyn, the big baby!"
"Mervyn, the wimp!"

You know, sometimes, I would prefer to be homeschooled. Except that, in my case, I would have to spend all my time with my dad, and that might be worse. Once, I tried to get something off my chest by talking to him, but in return I got:

"Mervyn, the big baby!" "Mervyn, the wimp!"

SOMETIMES, YOU JUST CAN'T WIN.

However, ever since I had detention with Mr. Bing, he's been super nice to me. It's funny, because it was supposed to be a punishment, but those training sessions were some of the best moments I've ever had. It almost makes me want to get into trouble so I can get detention again.

ALMOST.

Mr. Bing keeps giving me training advice for the championship. He told me that if I really want to impress the judges, I will have to come up with something they have never seen before— something so incredible, that everyone will keep talking about it for years to come.

Well, duh! Of course I have to do something incredible! My dad has been parroting the same thing for years. I don't even know anymore how many times he's told me the story of how he won three titles in a row.

One year, he lured a bunch of Minecraftians into the forest with a big pile of gold. Then he exploded right next to them. This is surely why you don't see any Minecraftians lurking about these parts nowadays. Since no one had ever used Minecraftians in a competition before, the judges gave my dad the maximum number of points for creativity. He received an overall score of 182 points, the highest score of all time.

The following year, he laid out a chain reaction in a very clever pattern, which he set off by exploding at one of the ends. The trees, the pigs—even the hills—he flipped them all upside down, one by one, with a single explosion. He was lucky in that the area was arranged in a way that made his chain possible—but, according to my dad, it's not a question of luck.

"You make your own luck, my boy," he repeats endlessly. But I don't believe it. I am one of the unluckiest creepers I know.

WHY WOULD I WANT TO MAKE MY OWN LUCK WHEN MY LUCK IS HORRIBLE?

DAY 16

I hate Wesley. No, that word is not strong enough.
I loathe him, I abhor him, I revile him.

He stole my diary! Wesley the weasel stole my
diary from me! And as if that weren't enough,
he brought it to school and read it out loud in
front of everybody.

"Oooh! Poor Mervyn! Poor, sensitive little creature!"
Weasley snickered as I tried to get the diary back.
"Give it back! It's private!"

I threw myself onto Wesley and knocked him
over, biting and hitting him—I was that furious.
He rolled on top of the notebook so I couldn't
grab it, and he crushed it in the process.

"GIVE ME MY DIARY!"

"Go on, worm. Keep trying," Wesley chortled, while I
tried to pull my notebook out from under him.

"That's enough, you two." Mr. Bing intervened to separate us. "Would you like to explain what's going on here?"

Wesley looked at me. I looked at Wesley.

Everyone knows you shouldn't be a tattletale. But he had my diary!

"Mr. Bing, Wesley stole my diary."

"That's not true!" Wesley exclaimed.

Mr. Bing shot Wesley a dark look. "Oh really? Give it here, Wesley."

Wesley sighed and handed over the diary. Mr. Bing took a quick glance inside.

"That's not your handwriting, Wesley. Mervyn, don't worry, I didn't read anything you wrote. But maybe you should choose more carefully where you leave your diary in the future. Wesley would not have been able to take it if you had paid closer attention. Either way, you know the rules about fighting. You are both getting detention. Together. Once I'm done with you, you will have learned how to work together. Or else you'll be in detention until you do."

He turned on his heel and left.

"You're going to regret having knocked me over, worm," Wesley said. He stuck his tongue out at me. "Keep your dumb diary. It's not as if you had anything interesting to write about, anyway. Your life is as boring as you are. See you in detention, loser!"

DAY 17

Being in detention with Wesley is hell. I would prefer to be thrown into a crater filled with ocelots rather than spend another minute with him. He annoys me so much!

"Very good, you two. I need your help moving some sports equipment. To begin with, take that chest and move it to the other side of the clearing."

Wesley and I looked at the chest and sighed. Those things weigh a ton. Since creepers don't have arms, it's super difficult to move things.

"Take the front, worm," ordered Wesley.

"No, you take the front," I replied.

"I'm stronger, so I should take the back."

"But I'm taller, so I should take the back."

"Wesley, take the back! Mervyn, take the front! Stop bickering, you two. There is a lot of work to be done and you are not going anywhere until you have finished."

Wesley threw me a satisfied smile and went to the back end of the chest. It wasn't fair. Even Mr. Bing was taking his side now.

We both stepped up to our ends and slid under the chest. Then we stood up, balancing the chest on our heads. When you don't have arms, you have to get creative if you want to move stuff.

"Go faster, worm!"

"I'm going as fast as I can! You slow down!"

"I can't slow down! I'll fall if I do!"

"Stop!"

"Keep going!"

"Humph!" Suddenly, Wesley dropped his end and the chest fell on my toes.

"Ow! That hurts!"

"If one of you damages my sports equipment,

you will be in serious trouble," growled Mr. Bing. "I suggest you stop acting like idiots and get to work. When you have finished with the chest, I want you to take care of the mats."

Wesley laughed to himself, and thinking Mr. Bing couldn't hear him mimicked him:

"If you make fun of Mervyn one more time, Wesley, I'll keep you in detention every day for a month ..."

Then reverting to himself, he said, "But Mr. Bing! The Creeper Combustion and Confusion Competition is barely a week away! I'll miss it if I am in detention—and everybody knows I'm the one who's going to win!"

"So you'd better behave, don't you think?" said Mr. Bing.

This time, I was the one who laughed.

DAY 18

I found a new hiding spot for my books. It's a little cave next to the lake. I got some stuff to make the cave look like an ocelot lair. Wesley can try to pretend he's not afraid of anything, but I know he's a scaredy-cat when it comes to ocelots. As are all creepers. Well, the ocelots do have very pointy teeth and very sharp claws.

The more I read these books, the more I think that creepers should be crafting more things. There are so many interesting creations to make. Why do we sleep outside, in the forest, when we could make comfortable beds for ourselves?

I asked my dad this question and he laughed in my face.

"Don't be an idiot, Mervyn. Creepers don't need

beds! We're very happy sleeping in the bushes."
"But dad," I protested. "Have you already tried sleeping in a bed?"

"Certainly not! I am a creeper! I would never do such a thing! So forget all this nonsense and concentrate on your training. Creepers don't build. Creepers destroy."

I'm not going to tell him that I've built myself a bed in the forest out of wood and wool. I had a crazy time trying to get that wool. I had to carefully arrange my explosions so that the wool fell off, but the sheep didn't blow up. I had to practice hard to master this, but I told myself it was a good exercise for the championship. After all, Mr. Bing has shown me just how much difference a well-placed explosion can make.

I don't understand why my dad doesn't want to try sleeping in a bed. It's so soft and so warm. It's much better than sleeping on the

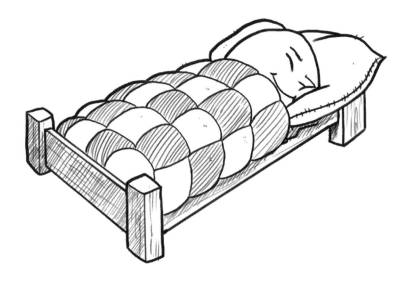

ground. But if I told him that I've made a bed,
I know he'd be furious with me. So I changed
the subject and asked him to tell me about
his competitions.

My dad can keep talking about his past victories
for hours.

DAY 19

Ever since Wesley stole my private diary, I don't want to talk about my training in here, in case he picks my diary up again.

ON THE OTHER HAND, NOTHING STOPS ME FROM TALKING ABOUT HIS TRAINING!

I had no intention of watching him train. I was smack in the middle of the forest looking for materials to use in crafting.

I came across a furnace in one of the books and thought that would be a cool thing to build.

If I set off an explosion in a furnace, it would catapult flaming logs in every direction. The fire would spread everywhere in the competition zone and everything would burn to the ground in seconds.

After all, it is called the Creeper Combustion and Confusion Competition. The rules only say you have to create destruction—they don't say how.

I didn't find what I was looking for, but, when I heard Wesley's voice, I plunged into the bushes to watch.

"Okay, guys," Wesley was saying. "Time me as I run around the clearing. I'm going to explode in each of the four corners, which should make the clearing twice as big as before."

I sank lower so that he wouldn't see me when he passed—and then I realized that if I stayed where I was, I was going to get blown up, too!

I began to crawl away, hoping he wouldn't see me.

"Hey! Hey! Look at the worm! He's running away by crawling on his stomach—like a good little earthworm should!"

I FROZE.

"Trying to pick up some tricks, worm?" Wesley came up to me from behind and gave me a kick. I turned around and looked him in the eyes.

"I don't blame you," he added. "I am super talented, after all."

He bent down and brought his head close to mine.

"At any rate, if you think you're going to steal my ideas so that you can win the competition, you're going to have to find something else to do. The judges don't like cheaters. And I will make sure that everybody knows you're a cheater."

"But I'm not cheating!" I protested. "I have my own plan, and it's better than yours."

"Oh yeah?"

Wesley didn't even bother to argue. He turned his back on me, laughing so hard that he nearly exploded.

DAY 20

They've started making the competition zones, so half the forest is now closed off.

I would like to be able to go and see what it is they're making, but I'm not allowed. It's strictly forbidden for competitors to see the zone that is reserved for them before the start of the competition. Those who try to sneak a peek will be disqualified on the spot.

I wonder what mine will look like. I hope there are a lot of trees.

You can do a ton of stuff with wood, and I already have an idea. **IT'S GOING TO BE THE BOMB!**

*Sometimes, I'm so funny that
I make myself laugh.*

DAY 21

It's so difficult to concentrate in school, with all the racket coming from the construction zone, that Mr. Bluebottle said we could have a break in our lessons and instead go play in the yard, under the supervision of the gym teacher.

"Wesley! Oscar! You'll be captains," Mr. Bing barked. "Pick your teams accordingly."

I hate it when they form teams like this. I am always the last to be chosen. And so, of course, when there was only me and Greg left at the end, Wesley chose Greg instead of me—even though we all know that Greg doesn't know how to run and that he is incapable of exploding correctly.

Every time he tries, he sneezes, and this makes one of his legs fall off.

"Okay, Mervyn. You're on Oscar's team. We'll be playing dodgeball. Now, remember, this game is intended for you to work on controlling your detonations. A creeper who explodes will make his team lose one point. If you explode three times, you're out for good. Wesley's team starts. Everybody to their positions... Ready, play!"

I hate dodgeball. Wesley always aims directly at me and he is truly talented with the ball.

I was nearly tempted to blow myself up three times straight so I could be eliminated, but I knew that the rest of my team would hate me for costing them so many points.

Wesley shot straight at my head. I did my best to duck, but the ball grazed me, anyway.

BOOM !

I couldn't help myself. I exploded.

"Mervyn! Your team loses a point. Get off the court."

I limped toward the bench, ignoring my teammates, who were glaring at me.

If only Mr. Bluebottle hadn't canceled our classes … I would have rather been in math, than be here, getting shot at by Wesley.

DAY 22

"Behind you, Mervyn! An ocelot!"

"AAAAAH!"

I didn't stop to turn around and make sure, and I didn't have the time to find a place to hide. I exploded, hoping I would take the ocelot with me.

I felt pretty silly once I'd respawned. There had been no ocelot, of course. If an ocelot had wandered into the forest, the creeper alarm would have gone off so that everyone could run for shelter.

"You're so stupid, worm!"
This was obviously a prank by Wesley and his crew.

"I'm almost sorry I didn't wait until the competition to do that to you," Wesley continued.

"It would have been pretty hilarious to see you explode in front of the judges. Did you see his face? This was the funniest thing to happen all day!"

I turned bright green as Wesley and his friends made a circle around me, chanting:

"Ocelots! Ocelots! Ocelots! Ocelots!"

"That's enough! Break it up!"

Mr. Bing broke into the center of our group, his eyes flashing. The others instantly shut up.

"Would someone have the decency to explain to me what is going on here?" growled Mr. Bing.

"We were just trying to help Mervyn, Mr. Bing," replied Wesley innocently. "He told us that he needed a hand in preparing for unexpected situations. So we pretended an ocelot was roaming in the forest."

"Is this true, Mervyn?"

I looked at Wesley, who raised his chin as a warning.

"Yes, Mr. Bing," I sighed. "I was starting to stress about the competition and I wanted to be sure that I could remain calm, no matter what happened."

Mr. Bing looked at us sideways, first at me, then at Wesley, and I knew that he didn't believe me. But he couldn't do anything if I didn't tell him the truth.

"Fine. If that is what you were doing, then, by all means, continue. But be less noisy from now on, okay?"

"Yes, Mr. Bing," we chorused as he left.

"Good job worm, you kept your mouth shut," Wesley sneered. "We all know what happens to little rats in the corner of the schoolyard."

I nodded and raised my eyes to the sky.

"You know what, Wesley? If I were you, I would be busy preparing for the competition, instead of worrying about what I'm coming up with."

"What a stupid worm!" Wesley laughed. "I'm way more prepared than you think. It's you who should be worried about what I'm coming up with."

DAY 23

I had the horrible feeling he was right.

"Come on, Mervyn. I want you to show me how you're going to win the competition."

My dad had brought me to a section of the forest where I don't usually go. I couldn't believe my eyes when I discovered that he had set up a training zone for me alone.

"It's a reconstruction of the zone where I had my third victory. You remember what I did, don't you?"

Did I remember? It's difficult to forget a story when my dad tells it nonstop, over and over again: how he leapt from hill to hill and set off a series of explosions to make the ground flat, and how he then ran to the center and buried himself so deep that, by the time he was finished with everything, the whole zone was completely the opposite of what it had been. The hills had become valleys and the valleys hills.

"I don't want you to do the same thing I did," my dad said. "I want you to find your own way of using the zone. Who knows, you may get the same layout, and you'll lose points if you foolishly copy me."

"Yes, Dad."

"Are you ready?

ON YOUR MARK...GET SET...
GO!"

I took a moment to stand still, like Mr. Bing taught me, in order to breathe a little and get an idea of the landscape.

"What are you waiting for, my boy? **MOVE!**"

I threw myself toward the center of the zone and exploded. But I hardly made a dent in the ground.

I scolded myself for having wasted time. I went to one of the hills and lay down at the bottom, thinking that if I blew up right there, I would create a landslide.

All I ended up doing was making a bunch of pebbles shake.

My dad hurried toward me.

"Stop, stop! I can't see any more of this. I can't believe I let you enter a competition for which you are so obviously unprepared."

"But Dad, I have a plan!" I protested. "Except I don't want to show it, in case someone steals my ideas."

"Mervyn, that's impossible. You cannot possibly have an idea so brilliant that someone will want to steal it from you. You're looking for excuses because you didn't notice the most effective places for detonating, here and here, which were obvious." He went to stand in the spot he indicated and then exploded, causing ten times more damage than my ridiculous explosions had.

"I'm sorry, Dad," I said. I lowered my head, ashamed.

"It's not to me that you need to apologize—it's to my fans, who are looking forward to finding out how good my son is. You're going to let a lot of people down if you believe that this is good enough for the championship. **HUMPH!**"

He left in a fury, leaving me standing there.

Was this the right thing to do—wait for the competition to try out my plan? Maybe I should have trained more, and not have worried so much about whether or not Wesley was spying on me.

In any case, it was too late to change anything now.

DAY 24

The championship starts tomorrow, and I am so stressed out, I've exploded four times. The first time was at breakfast. My dad was so mad at me that he sent me outside, telling me not to come back before I was capable of controlling my detonations again.

"How do you think you're going to win tomorrow if you can't even eat your breakfast without blowing up?" my dad raged. "Keep this up and you won't even be ranked. I'm warning you right now, if you embarrass me, I will not be pleased. You must preserve my legacy. I will not tolerate being humiliated by my son."

Well, thanks, Dad.
Way to add more pressure.

I walked in the forest to try to relax. Usually,

making my way to the lake calms me down. On the path, however, I heard Wesley joking around with his friends, so I took a detour. The last thing I needed today was to bump into him.

How can he be so relaxed, when the competition is tomorrow morning?

It's also his first time competing, so I'd hoped he'd at least be a little stressed, too.

Except that he has friends to tell him how awesome he's going to be. As for me, nobody seems to think I'll do well. If my plan fails, then they'll be proven right. But I know my idea is a good one—even if no other creeper has ever tried to do what I'm planning to do tomorrow.

It's hard to train. Without knowing what's in my zone, I can't figure how to best use my resources. But I've read and reread the library books until I know them by heart, and I know that if I don't panic and take my time to study the zone, I will make competition history.

DAY 25

"Ladies and gentlemen, boys and girls, welcome to the 102nd annual Creeper Combustion and Confusion Competition!"

Edward Hewitt announced the opening of the championship to thunderous applause. I was in the row reserved for competitors, nervously hopping from one foot to the other as we waited for the parade to begin. We were going to march through the forest and finally see all the competition zones.

"It's not too late to back out, worm," teased Wesley. "You're looking like you need your mommy. Maybe you should go now, before everyone makes fun of you. Since I'm in a generous mood, I'll forget our bet if you drop out. You'll never get a better deal than this—I suggest you take it."

"Why? You scared of losing?" I retorted.

Wesley opened his mouth to reply, but he was cut off by a series of exploding creepers, who were setting off a fireworks salute into the sky. The parade had begun!

I couldn't believe that I was finally participating in the competition. I had dreamed of this moment my entire life. I had a smile on my face, waving to the crowd as we went through the

forest and passed the competition zones, each of which was assigned to a different competitor. When we got to my zone, Wesley laughed loudly.

"There's nothing to destroy! You should have withdrawn when you had the chance."

Looking over the zone, I could see what he meant.

My zone was not at all how I would have liked it to be. There was a lot of rubble and an entrance to an abandoned mine. It would have presented a problem to most creepers. However, I knew that my plan could still work, so I tried to play it cool.

"Speak for yourself, Wesley. Just because you're not talented enough to win doesn't mean I'm not."

The parade ended with a huge celebration in honor of all the participants. But, despite the banquet of delicious food, I was far too nervous to swallow anything.

"What's wrong, worm? Second thoughts?"

Wesley was stuffing his face with pumpkin pie.

"Enjoy your meal," I advised him. "Because, in a few days, you're going to be eating humble pie."

"You'd like that, huh?"

Wesley threw a slice of pie at me, which hit me straight in the face. I narrowed my eyes and hissed, but I stopped myself from throwing something at him in return. With my bad luck, I told myself, I would be accused of having started the fight, even though it was Wesley's fault, and then I would be disqualified from the competition before I even had a chance to show what I was capable of.

DAY 26

There are so many competitors that the championship will last three days. This morning we drew straws to find out the order we would be going in, and I got the last slot.

"That's good," my dad said. "This way you will have seen the performances of all the other participants, and you will know how many points you need to win the title. The one who goes first never wins. I feel sorry for the poor creeper who gets that slot."

My dad and I were on the sidelines, watching creepers giving it their all, one after the other, as they tried to impress the judges.

"There's a bunch of talented creepers here," I gulped, as I saw a competitor transform a hill into a crater in a single explosion. I hadn't realized just how good everyone would be.

"What did you expect, Mervyn? This is the Creeper Combustion and Confusion Competition. Only the best of the best take part," my dad replied, turning toward me. "Are you sure you want to do this? It's not too late to forfeit. You could always make up for it next year, you know."

First Wesley and now my dad.

Aside from them, is anyone interested in watching me compete, or not?

By the end of the day, the competition had been so fierce that there was only a five-point difference between the three creepers in the lead.

"Currently in first place is Marcus Sparks," Edward Hewitt announced to the crowd, which was going wild. "Will anyone attempt to beat his score of 168 points? We will find out tomorrow."

DAY 27

Today was Wesley's turn. He took his position at the edge of his zone. Was I mistaken, or did he look a little more green than usual?

"TAKE YOUR MARK... GET SET ... GO!"

As the gun went off, Wesley exploded! The crowd laughed, and I felt much more relieved.

If Wesley was so stressed as to jump at the smallest noise, then he wasn't going to do all that well.

I was finally going to win our bet.

Wesley respawned and set out to do a round of

his zone at full speed. My heart was in my throat as I watched him run. Even though he'd had a bad start, he made up for lost time, and, when he stopped, his zone was completely flattened and there was nothing left to destroy... And there were still ten minutes left on the timer.

"He'll gain extra points for that," my dad said

to me. "That was very impressive—almost as fast as I was in my time."

Obviously, no one would ever be as good as my dad had been in his time, but it still bothered me a lot to hear him praise Wesley like that.
"At the end of the second day of the Creeper

Combustion and Confusion Competition, it's Wesley Kaffarnaum who takes the lead with an overall score of 198, out of 200 possible points," Edward Hewitt announced. "Tomorrow's participants will have to outdo themselves to beat this!"

Wesley caught hold of me as he passed by. "I told you that you should have dropped out when you had the chance," he taunted. "But don't worry. Your T-shirt is ready, it's waiting for you, and I've been stocking fruit for weeks. When I am done with you, you're going to be leaking rotten fruit."

He disappeared into the crowd, surrounded by his admirers. They were all acting as if Wesley had already won the championship. And, I had to admit, with a score like that—he probably had.

DAY 28

I didn't sleep last night. I could not stop
thinking about what I was going to do in the
competition. I had been preparing for this since
forever, and, now that the big day was here,
I couldn't help thinking that my plans were
terrible. It seemed impossible that I could win.

The worst thing was that I was the last to
go, so I was going to have to watch all the
other competitors try to beat Wesley's score—
and fail. Some of them had been doing this
competition for years and had mastered their
technique perfectly.

If creepers chock-full of talent couldn't beat Wesley, what chance did I have?

"And now, here is our final competitor," Edward
Hewitt announced. "Please welcome to the arena

the son of Big Raymundo–Mervyn Miles!"

The crowd cheered and applauded. I froze in fear. Why did he have to remind everyone who my dad was? Now I was going to look even more like an idiot when I messed up.

"Go ahead, Mervyn. Take your mark." My dad pushed me halfway, and then I finally remembered how to use my legs. I positioned myself at the entrance to the mine. It was dark and not very inviting in there.

I looked around me, searching for a sign that could help me in my quest for destruction. Unfortunately, the zone held nothing special outside of the gaping hole that led into the mine. In fact, I was even at a disadvantage compared to the other creepers. There was nothing here except trees and rocks, scattered in the worst possible way. The mine was my only hope.

"TAKE YOUR MARK... GET SET ...
GO!"

At the sound of the gun, I threw myself into the mine. The spectators murmured in surprise. Usually, when a creeper encounters a mine in his zone, he blows up the entrance to block it. This

is worth a lot of points.

Except, I was more ambitious than that. I knew exactly what I was looking for, but I wasn't sure I would find it in time. We hadn't been allowed to explore our zones in detail before the start of the competition, but I hoped to get my hands on the things I needed before my allotted time ran out.

I plunged deeper and deeper into the mine.

"Come on, come on, where are you?"

It was useless. The things I needed weren't here. I knew my chances of coming across the remains of TNT were very small.

BUT CAN YOU IMAGINE HOW BIG THE EXPLOSION WOULD BE, IF I BLEW MYSELF UP ON A PILE OF TNT?

But I also hoped to find a little bit of redstone or some diamonds.

This mine had been abandoned for one very good reason, though. Everything that could be useful had already been carried out. It was impossible for me to win; but at least I could get back some points by destroying some trees.

I was going to give up and leave the mine— when I realized that the answer was right there under my very nose. All the books I read mentioned what could be crafted out of the most basic things. But I had been so preoccupied with wanting to create something exceptional that I had missed the most obvious thing:

BLOCKS OF STONE!

I calculated the best place to explode and got into position.

BOOM!

I was ejected out of the mineshaft, flying through the air like a firework. I saw the other creepers watching me with their mouths hanging open.

When I landed, I started to run in every direction to gather the blocks.

No creeper in the history of the Creeper Combustion and Confusion Competition had ever built anything, and the usually noisy crowd watched in complete silence as I built a stone castle

Once my castle was finished, I glanced at the timer. I didn't have a lot of time left to put the rest of my plan into action, so I didn't waste a single second to stop and admire my handiwork. I rushed inside the castle.

I stood upright in the very center, ready to explode. I wasn't going to make an ordinary explosion.

I HAD BIG PLANS FOR MY CASTLE.

I started to spin around and around to gather energy, more and more—and then I released the biggest explosion of my entire life.

BOOM ! BANG ! BOOM !

My castle was demolished into a million pieces. Blocks of stone flew through the sky, then shattered on the ground to create a magnificent stone garden. I picked one flower that bloomed next to me and I placed it on top of a stone block, just before the final whistle blew.

I turned to face the audience. Silence.

That was not the reaction I was expecting.

Then, suddenly, the crowd started to clap and to cheer.

"Bravo, Mervyn!"

"Well played, Mervyn!"

"You're the best, Mervyn!"

I blushed and turned toward the judges, waiting for them to announce my score.

"And Mervyn Miles' score is ...197 points out of 200. The winner of this year's Creeper Combustion and Confusion Competition is Wesley Kaffarnaum!"

My heart dropped. Wesley won? After all my efforts, Wesley beat me anyway?

"Bad luck, worm," sneered Wesley, shoving me out of the way as he went to get his crown.

Mr. Bing, who had been one of the judges, came over to me.

"I'm so sorry, Mervyn," he said. "I tried to convince the other judges that you should be the winner, but one of them took off points because you had crafted something. He said that if you had indeed pulverized a castle, then that would have been groundbreaking for the championship. But you built a castle and then left behind a garden—that's what he penalized you for. Still, you should be proud of yourself. You did very well."

"But not well enough," murmured my dad, who was standing behind me.

I have to admit he was right.

DAY 29

"I AM A BIG LOSER."

Feeling defeated, I looked at the words written across my T-shirt.

Why had I made that dumb bet? As if it weren't enough that I would have to endure Wesley for the whole year while he crowed about his victory. Now I had to walk through the entire forest in this T-shirt so everyone could make fun of me.

Sighing, I slipped on the T-shirt and set out to look for Wesley. My dad caught up with me while I was walking.

"What are you doing in that ridiculous T-shirt? Take it off at once!"

"I can't," I replied. "I made a bet with Wesley. He won the competition, so I have to wear this."

"What are you talking about? Haven't you heard?"

"Heard what?"

"Wesley cheated! He went inside the zone before the competition so he could figure out how best to use the space to create the biggest possible explosions. He's been disqualified. That means you won, Mervyn! You won!"

I couldn't believe it.

I ripped off the T-shirt and followed my dad to where the judges had gathered.

"Mervyn!" Mr. Bing smiled. "I have the pleasure of

declaring you the winner of this year's Creeper Combustion and Confusion Competition."

"How? I mean, I don't understand. How did Wesley cheat?"

"He disguised himself as a worker to gain access to his zone so he could think about the best ways to destroy it. I must admit I had my doubts when I saw his performance. Wesley had always been good in practice, but not that good. You were the one who always had an inventive streak—the gift of looking at things in an original way."

"But how did he get caught? He must have been roaming in the zone for weeks. Why did it take so long to uncover this?"

"Wesley's worst enemy is Wesley himself," Mr. Bing explained. "He would have gotten away with it, if he hadn't said anything. He would still be champion—but he could not hold his tongue. One of the judges heard him boasting to his friends. He was telling them he had figured out how, by exploding in the right place, he could easily destroy half of his zone—but then he very nearly ruined everything by blowing up in the wrong place. He explained to his friends that, had he not managed to examine his zone before the competition, he never would have found that right place, and that the other creepers were pretty foolish not to have done the same thing."

"WHOA! I never thought Wesley would do this."

"Do what? Cheat, or tell everybody that he had cheated?"

Mr. Bing and I both smiled hugely.

"Both."

"In any case, he did do both. And now the best creeper wins. Come on. Everyone is waiting for you to get on the podium.

"It's time you receive the prize you deserve.

131

"That castle was incredible, you know. It's almost a shame you had to destroy it. Maybe one day you can show me how you did it."

"I would like that very much."

Mr. Bing led me to the podium where Edward Hewitt and the other judges were waiting for me. When Edward placed the winner's crown on my head, I thought I would explode with joy. But the surprises weren't over.

"Now that we have the opportunity to look at the scores in detail, you should also know that you have joined your father on the list of record-breakers," said Edward. "You received more points than any competitor in the history of the championship."

My dad climbed up on the podium to pat me on the shoulder.

"Well done, my boy. I'm proud of you."

I never thought I would hear him say those words. I was the happiest of creepers.

DAY 30

There is nothing better in the world than winning the Creeper Combustion and Confusion Competition. Walking through the forest, I felt as if I were walking on air!

Every time I met someone, I had to stop, say hello, and sign an autograph—it took me an hour to get to school instead of the usual five minutes.

When I walked through the school doors, Mr. Bluebottle, the principal, was waiting to congratulate me.

"Mervyn," he said, smiling. "Our big winner. I decree that everyone gets the day off today to celebrate your victory."

All the students cheered:

"Hip, hip, hurray for Mervyn!"

I looked at all the happy, smiling faces surrounding me—but there was one missing.

"Where's Wesley?" I asked.

Mr. Bluebottle looked out at the crowd with a distracted smile. "He's not here. I wouldn't be surprised if he was so ashamed of being caught cheating that he left the forest completely."

I was a little disappointed that Wesley hadn't stuck around to honor his end of our bet, but I couldn't blame him. If I were ever caught cheating, I, too, would want to run somewhere far away. And if he was gone for good—well, even better. I wouldn't have to put up with being called "worm" anymore.

At any rate, I didn't have time to worry about Wesley because the other creepers had raised me on their shoulders and were carrying me around the schoolyard, chanting, "Mervyn! Mervyn! Mervyn!" They were even talking about building a statue of me and putting it in the center of the yard, so everyone would have a reminder of my magnificent castle.

I was the most popular creeper in school. I couldn't keep myself from smiling. If they think what I'd done was awesome—wait until they see what I have planned for next year!

LOoK FOR:

AN UNOFFICIAL **MINECRAFT** DIARY

ADVENTURES OF A SLIME

Slibertius, the slime who wants to be a fashion designer!

↖ I will revolutionize fashion

BY BOOKS KID